Pepi
Sings a New Song

Laura Ljungkvist

Beach Lane Books

New York London Toronto Sydney

Pepi the parrot lived with Peter.

Peter loved space.

Every night while Peter stargazed,

Pepi sang him a special space song.

Twinkle, twinkle, little stars,
Satellite, planet, galaxy, Mars.

Comet, Venus, telescope,
Jupiter, rocket, Asterope.

Saturn, Mercury, Milky Way,
Neptune, orbit, moon, sun ray.

Pepi loved singing,
but Peter seemed a little tired of his song.
So Pepi decided to go find
some new things to sing about.

His first stop was . . .

Manuel's bakery!

"Hello, Pepi!" said Manuel.

"Would you like to find all the tasty things in my bakery?"

Soon Pepi had batches of tasty things to sing about.
So his next stop was . . .

Clive's music studio!

"**Hello, Pepi!**" said Clive.

"Would you like to find all the musical things in my studio?"

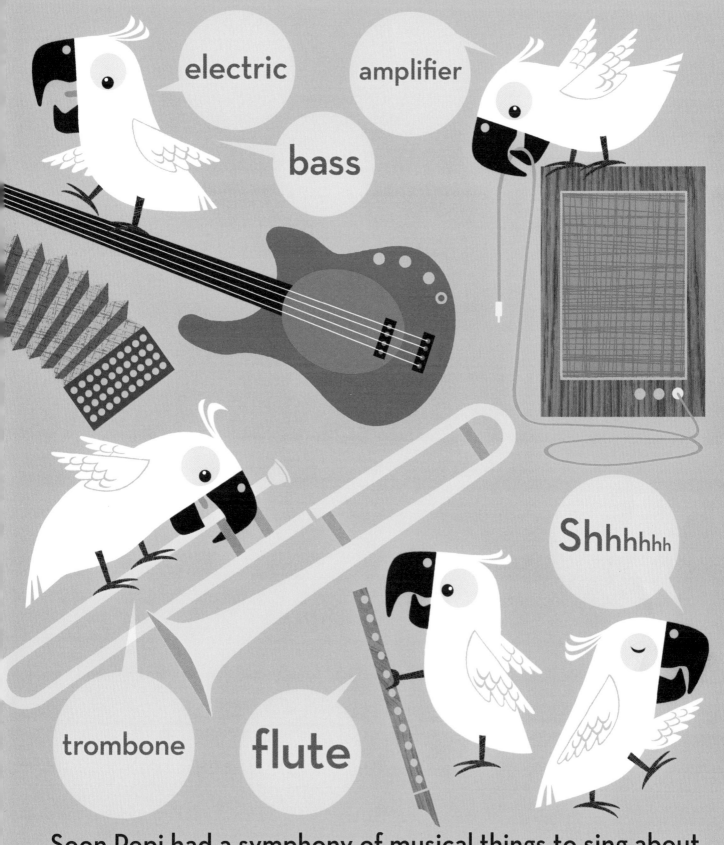

Soon Pepi had a symphony of musical things to sing about.

So his next stop was . . .

Aurora's art studio!

"Hello, Pepi!" said Aurora.

"Would you like to find all the creative things in my studio?"

Soon Pepi had a collage of creative things to sing about.
So his next stop was . . .

Malcolm's market!

"Hello, Pepi!" said Malcolm.

"Would you like to find all the hearty things in my market?"

Soon Pepi had a harvest of hearty things to sing about.
So his next stop was . . .

Cynthia's dog park!

"Hello, Pepi!" said Cynthia.

"Would you like to find all the puppy things in my park?"

Soon Pepi had a pack of puppy things to sing about.
So his next stop was . . .

Pepi's new song was ready.

And he couldn't wait to sing it for Peter.

Twinkle, twinkle, little flute,
Poodle, xylophone, cobalt, fruit.

Carrot, saxophone, icing, bow,
Violet, terrier, canvas, dough.

Pastries, whippet, sculpture, kale,
Bulldog, easel, trombone, scale.

Pepi's song was a hit.
And Peter was inspired!
So now every night
Pepi and Peter sing their
special new song . . .

together!

Twinkle, twinkle . . .

In loving memory of Minnie

**Special thanks to Rebecca Sherman and the Beach Lane ladies
and especially to Paul and Violet for their genius contributions**

BEACH LANE BOOKS · An imprint of Simon & Schuster Children's Publishing Division · 1230 Avenue of the Americas, New York, New York 10020 · Copyright © 2010 by Laura Ljungkvist · All rights reserved, including the right of reproduction in whole or in part in any form. · BEACH LANE BOOKS is a trademark of Simon & Schuster, Inc. · For information about special discounts for bulk purchases, please contact Simon & Schuster Special Sales at 1-866-506-1949 or business@simonandschuster.com · The Simon & Schuster Speakers Bureau can bring authors to your live event. For more information or to book an event, contact the Simon & Schuster Speakers Bureau at 1-866-248-3049 or visit our website at www.simonspeakers.com. · Book design by Lauren Rille · The text for this book is set in Neutraface Text. · The illustrations for this book are rendered digitally. · Manufactured in China · First Edition · 2 4 6 8 10 9 7 5 3 1 · Library of Congress Cataloging-in-Publication Data · Ljungkvist, Laura. · Pepi sings a new song / Laura Ljungkvist.—1st ed. · p. cm. · Summary: Pepi the parrot goes exploring and discovers a whole wide world of new words to sing about. · ISBN 978-1-4169-9138-0 (hardcover : alk. paper) · [1. Parrots—Fiction. 2. Vocabulary—Fiction.] I. Title. · PZ7.L7657Pe 2010 · [E]—dc22 · 2009016476